Scurry's New Neighbor

Tharini Pande

Illustrated by Lex Avellino

TRAITMARKER BOOKS

TRAITMARKER BOOKS
2984 Del Rio Pike
Franklin, TN 37069

Ordering Information for Quantity Sales:
Special discounts are available on quantity purchases by corporations, associations, and others.
For details, contact the author at the address above.

Interior Text Font: Open Dyslexic
Title Font: Jazz Ball
Illustrator: Alexander Avellino
Editor: Robbie Grayson III
Cover Design: Katherine Grayson

Book Publishing Information:
ISBN 978-1-944781-71-2
Published by TRAITMARKER BOOKS
traitmarkerbooks.com traitmarker@gmail.com
Printed in the United States of America

To Aarna and Yuv, my greatest inspiration.

T.P.

The branches of the tall Oak
tree danced to the tunes
of the whistling wind.

Safely nestled inside a deep hole in the tree was a fluffy red squirrel. Scurry let out a sigh as he stretched from head to tail, knowing that he had work to do.

"Is that singing coming from my tree?" squeaked Scurry as he stretched his neck.

Scurry had always had the Oak tree all to himself. But now there she was with her bright white face and the most magnificent blue that he had ever seen across her wings and back.

"All the nuts around the tree are mine," whined Scurry at the thought of having to share.

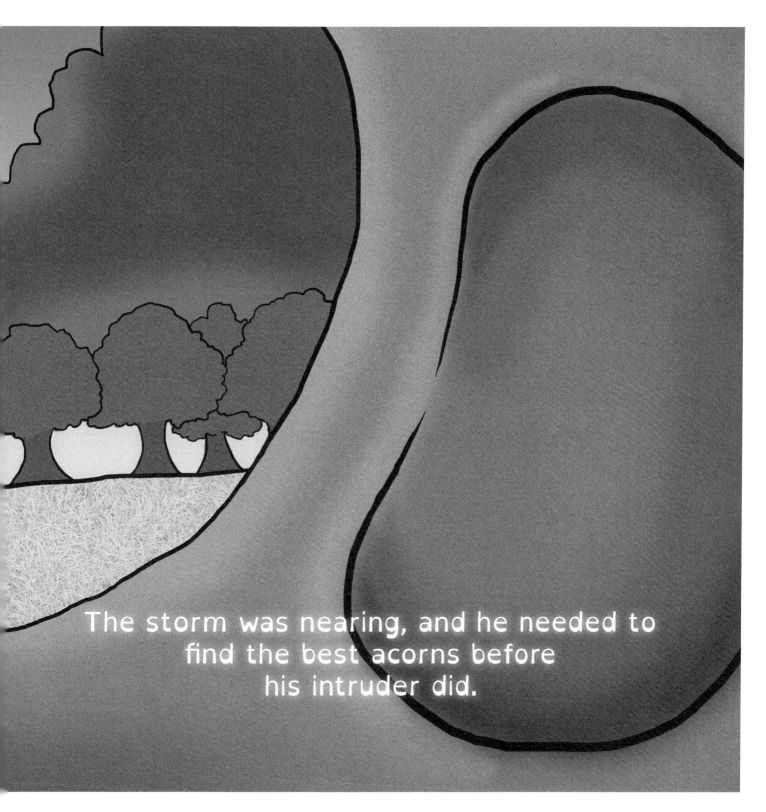

The storm was nearing, and he needed to
find the best acorns before
his intruder did.

Scurry first picked a green acorn and sniffed hard at it. The fresh bitter scent made his stomach churn, but the nut felt a little soft.

Lying on a bed of weeds was a crisp brown acorn. Scurry's tongue sprung in and out as it grazed the smooth shell and breathed in its woody scent.

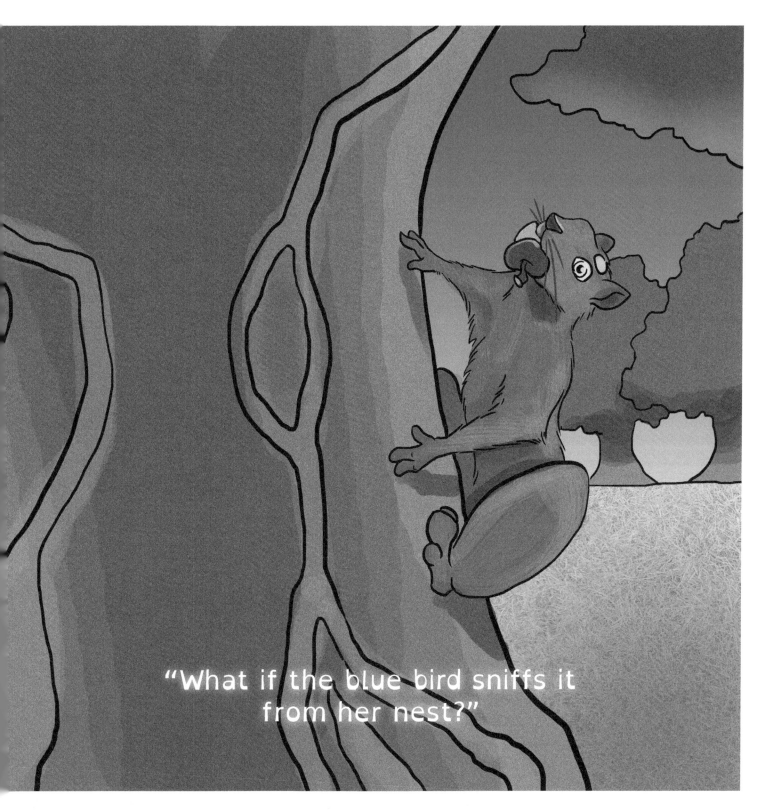

He needed to find a very special place to hide his food. But no hiding place seemed safe enough.

The wind was picking up strength and the rain was coming down harder.

Hungry, he headed home. He could see the blue bird snuggled in her nest.

Curled in a corner with his tail wrapped around him like a present, he hoped his tree would rock him to sleep.

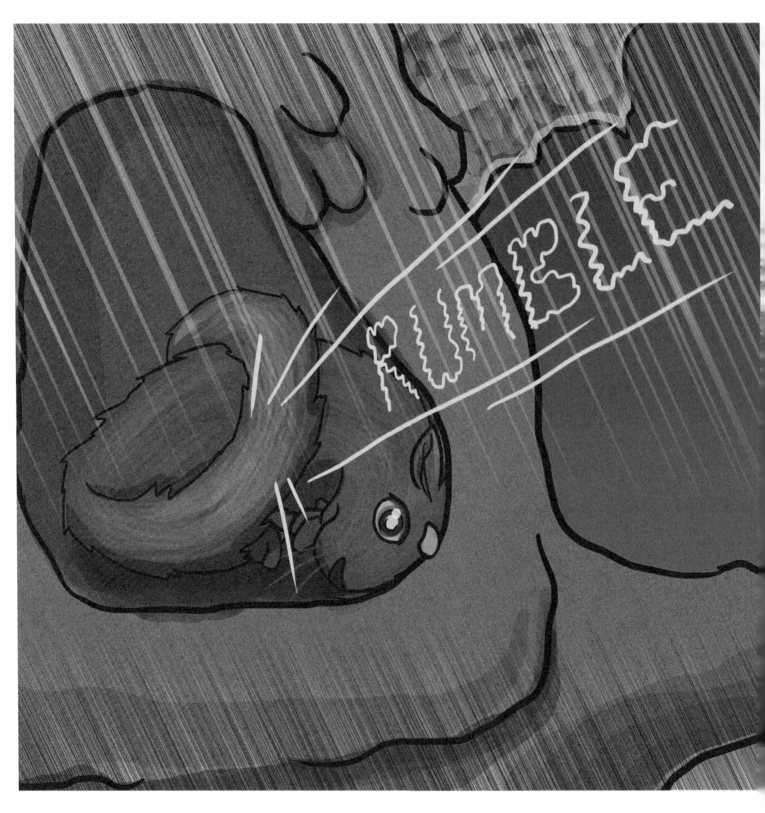

But his stomach
was louder than the storm.

"Thank you, blue bird. You are very kind," said Scurry, wishing he had not been so quick to judge.

TO THE PARENTS
On the Power of Sharing

Children are afraid to share. Whether it be at home, at school, or at the park, we parents always seem to be trying to get our children to share. Imparting the concept that selfishness is a losing battle can be a challenging task. Reiterating the beauty and power of sharing through colorful illustrations and characters with which every child is familiar can have a positive impact.

I read the story of Scurry and Blue-wy to my daughter for the first time when she was three years old, and I vividly remember her reaction as the story concluded. With a smile she said, "I'm so happy that Scurry found such a nice friend." It wasn't the thought of winning or losing with which she was left, but, rather, the importance of friendship.

We've all grown up hearing the popular proverb "Birds of a feather flock together." While this is a true, superficial observation, it is up to us to recognize the evolving world around us and to adapt our views accordingly. To understand that a creature - be it furry or feathered - ultimately has the same basic needs as others and to accept that we each can coexist peacefully despite our differences: *that* is to believe that this world is not just yours or mine, but ours.

Cheers!

Tharini Pande

CPSIA information can be obtained
at www.ICGtesting.com
Printed in the USA
LVOW05*1452210316
480092LV00035B/325/P